THREE KINGS, ONE NIGHT

Lost Kings MC #2.5

AUTUMN JONES LAKE

COPYRIGHT

Three Kings, One Night
Lost Kings MC #2.5
A Lost Kings MC Holiday
Copyright 2014 Autumn Jones Lake
All Rights Reserved
Digital ISBN: 978-1-943950-49-2
Print ISBN: 978-1-943950-02-7
Cover Designed by: AJ Lake
Stock Photo Adobe Stock

ALSO BY AUTUMN JONES LAKE

THE LOST KINGS MC™ SERIES

Slow Burn (Lost Kings MC #1)– *Free ebook!*

Corrupting Cinderella (Lost Kings MC #2)

Three Kings, One Night (Lost Kings MC #2.5)

Strength From Loyalty (Lost Kings MC #3)

Tattered on My Sleeve (Lost Kings MC #4)

White Heat (Lost Kings MC #5)

Between Embers (Lost Kings MC #5.5)

More Than Miles (Lost Kings MC #6)

White Knuckles (Lost Kings MC #7)

Beyond Reckless (Lost Kings MC #8)

Beyond Reason (Lost Kings MC #9)

One Empire Night (Lost Kings MC #9.5)

After Burn (Lost Kings MC #10)

After Glow (Lost Kings MC #11)

Zero Hour (Lost Kings MC #11.5) - *Free ebook!*

Zero Tolerance (Lost Kings MC #12)

Zero Regret (Lost Kings MC #13)

Zero Apologies (Lost Kings MC #14)

White Lies (Lost Kings MC #15)

Swagger and Sass (A Lost Kings MC Novella) - *Free ebook!*

Rhythm of the Road (Lost Kings MC #16)

Lyrics on the Wind (Lost Kings MC #17)

Diamond in the Dust (Lost Kings MC #18)

Crown of Ghosts (Lost Kings MC #19)

Throne of Scars (Lost Kings MC #20)

Reckless Truths (Lost Kings MC #21)

...and many more to come!

BOOKS IN THE LOST KINGS MC WORLD
The Hollywood Demons Series

Kickstart My Heart

Blow My Fuse

Wheels of Fire

Bullets & Bonfires

Warnings & Wildfires

Renegade Path

Paranormal Romance

Catnip & Cauldrons

Onyx Night

Onyx Shadows

Feral Escape

Dear Reader,

   Three Kings, One Night is a collection of three short stories (each one approximately 5,000 words). If you *don't* enjoy short stories because they are not long enough, then this is not the collection for you.

   If you *do* love short stories or you just want as much information about your favorite Lost Kings MC characters as you can get, then *welcome!*

   Inside, you'll find a sweet story about Murphy, the Road Captain of the Lost Kings MC. He wants to do something sweet for his best friend's little sister, Heidi, but ends up torturing himself instead.

   Then there's Wrath and Trinity. The club's enforcer and the club's house mama. No one really knows why they're so hostile toward each other, but for one night they set their animosity aside.

Finally, there's a steamy story about Zero and Lilly. Z stops by Lilly's house unannounced to bring her a sweet surprise.

Timeline:

Both Murphy's story and Wrath's story take place in between Parts 1 and 2 of Slow Burn (Lost Kings MC #1)

Z's story takes place after Corrupting Cinderella (Lost Kings MC #2)

Enjoy!

Autumn

GLOSSARY

If you've purchased this little Christmas book, I assume you're a fan of the series, so welcome back to the world of the Lost Kings MC! I first used a Glossary in the *Road to Royalty* boxed set. I thought it might be helpful to have some of the things specific to LOKI mentioned here ahead of time.

The Lost Kings MC Organizational Structure

President: *Rochlan "Rock" North.* Leader of the Upstate NY charter of the Lost Kings MC. The word of the President is law within the club. He takes advice from senior club members. He is the public "face" of the MC.

Sergeant-at-Arms: *Wyatt "Wrath" Ramsey.*

Responsible for the security of the club. Keeps order at club events. Responsible for the safety and protection of the president, the club, its members and its women. Disciplines club members who violate the rules. Keeps track of club by-laws. Will challenge Rock when he deems it necessary.

Vice President: *Zero or "Z".* In most clubs, I think the VP would be considered the second-in-command. In mine, I see the VP and SAA on equal footing within the club. Carries out the orders of the President. Communicates with other chapters of the club. Assumes the responsibilities of the President in his absence. Keeps records of club patches and colors issued.

Treasurer: *Marcel "Teller" Whelan.* Keeps records of income, expenses and investments.

Road Captain: *Blake "Murphy" O'Callaghan.* Responsible for researching, planning and organizing club runs. Responsible for obtaining and maintaining club vehicles.

The Lost Kings MC Ladies

Hope Kendal, Esq.: The object of Rock's love and obsession. Their epic love story spans four books; *Slow Burn, Corrupting Cinderella, Strength From Loyalty*, and soon-to-be-released *White Heat*.

Trinity Hurst: Caretaker of the Lost Kings MC clubhouse and the brothers. She and Wrath have a long, tattered love story full of lust, fury, and forgiveness in *Tattered on My Sleeve (Lost Kings MC #4)*

Heidi Whelan: Teller's little sister. Has nurtured a crush on her brother's best friend, Murphy, since she was a little girl. You get glimpses of Heidi through *Corrupting Cinderella, Strength From Loyalty, Tattered on My Sleeve, and White Heat*. She will have her own book, tentatively titled *On the Edge (Lost Kings MC #6)*, to be released sometime in 2016.

Lilly: One of Hope's best friends and frequent booty call of Z. She will be featured in *Zero Tolerance (Lost Kings MC #7)*.

Lost Kings MC Terminology

Crystal Ball – the strip club owned by the Lost Kings MC and one of their legitimate businesses. They often refer to it as just "CB".

"Conference Center" – the clubhouse of the Lost Kings MC. It was previously used as a conference center and is sometimes jokingly referred to this way.

Empire – The fictional city in Upstate NY, run by the Lost Kings.

Green Street Crew – Street gang the Lost Kings does business with. Often referred to as "GSC."

LOKI – short for Lost Kings.

Vipers MC – Rival and frequent enemy MC. Runs Ironworks which borders the Lost Kings Territory.

Wolf Knights MC – Rival and sometimes ally of the Lost Kings.

DEDICATION

Dedicated to fans of the Lost Kings MC.

MURPHY & HEIDI

CHAPTER ONE

MURPHY

"Bug, hand me that last strand of lights."

"No."

Heidi's tone makes me tip my head up and I accidentally jam a staple into my thumb. "Fuck, God dammit, Heidi!"

"Oh shit, Blake! I'm sorry."

I don't know why something so little hurts so fucking much, but it does. Feeling like an asshole for making such a big deal, I shake it off.

"Are you okay?" she asks.

Now I feel like a jerk for yelling at her. "Yeah, I'm fine. Hand me the lights?"

She does without complaining this time, and I manage to tack them up without further injury.

"Shoulda done this a fuckin' month ago, not Christmas Eve."

Heidi shrugs. "Grandma always goes out with her friends and then to church. She won't be back for a few hours."

Great, just what I need. Alone time with my best friend's hot, underage sister.

"Where's your dickhead brother?"

"Said he'd be over with some pizzas in a little bit."

Thank God.

"Want to come inside and help me hang stuff in there?"

Unfortunately, I do. That's why I will stay right the fuck out here where it's cold and we're in plain sight.

"No," I bark at her a little harsher than I intended. Her face falls and I want to punch myself.

"Sorry, Bug. I just want to finish this before it gets dark."

"Okay." She grabs an armful of garlands and starts twirling them around the porch railings.

"That front step still holding okay?"

Heidi bounces up and down on said step. "Yup."

Teller and I spent a good chuck of time and money last summer fixing up the outside of his grandmother's ancient Victorian house. Not that the old bat appreciated it, but Heidi deserved to live somewhere where the front porch wasn't crumbling apart.

"All right. Go flip the switch for me, Heidi-girl."

I laugh as she skips up the steps to get the lights. Then I'm blinded by the dozens of LED bulbs that come to life.

Heidi

The front porch bathed all in white Christmas lights is breathtaking. Spending time with Blake putting them up, has been perfect.

I've always been a sucker for Christmas lights. Grandma hates them. Well, she doesn't like the work, which at her age I understand.

"Thanks for helping me, Blake."

He rubs a hand over his tidy, ginger beard. "No problem, Bug."

God, how I hate when he calls me that. "You know what I'd like for Christmas?"

"What?"

"You to stop calling me bug."

He cocks his head, studying me before answering. Between his knit cap and facial hair, I can barely see him. "You know you can't pick your road name. You think I liked getting tagged with Murphy?"

Yes, I think he did like it. "I'm not part of the MC, so I don't need a road name."

"You're MC family."

Pretending I'm fixing one of the garlands, I reach down and grab a handful of snow and roll it into a quick ball.

"Don't you dare, Bug."

The snow makes a nice wet, whapping sound when I peg him in the chest with it.

"Now you're gonna get it."

He bends over and starts scooping up a massive amount of snow. No way am I getting pelted with one of his fastballs. Squealing, I turn and run in the opposite direction, around the house.

But Blake knows me too well. He must have gone the opposite way, because when I turn the corner, we collide and go down to the ground in a pile of limbs. Blake lets out a soft whoosh of air when I hit him. His arms instinctively wrap around me to protect me from the fall. I've got him pinned under me and I'm laughing so hard I can't get a breath.

"Damn girl, you're a friggin' linebacker."

"Funny."

"Get off me."

His arms are still wrapped around me, so I try and wriggle out of his hold. "I can't. Let go of me."

A strange look crosses his face, but he lifts his arms, laying them on the ground like he's about to make snow angels.

He grunts when I use his chest to push myself up.

A wet ball of snow pelts my cheek.

"Dammit, Blake! That went right down my jacket."

"Let's get you inside, before you freeze."

CHAPTER TWO

MURPHY

I DIDN'T *WANT* to be alone in the house with Heidi. But it turned out being *outside* with her was just as dangerous to my sanity.

Having her land on top of me had not improved my mental state at all. It almost made me do something I'd regret. After I shuck my wet coat, I turn around and am struck stupid.

Fuck me, what the hell is she wearing?

I'm used to seeing Heidi in baggy flannel shirts, hooded sweatshirts, and crap like that. Can't leave a sweatshirt around the girl, 'cause she'll steal it. I've lost too many to her thieving hands to count over the years.

So when she strips off her puffy winter coat, and then her sweatshirt, all she's left wearing is a long-sleeved thermal shirt. A thin shirt that clings to all the curves I'd been trying damn hard not to notice she'd developed.

Fuck.

A long-sleeved thermal shirt is about to make me lose my mind.

Why me?

"I should get going. Your grandmother will be back soon..."

Heidi turns to glance at the clock, and Christ, I can't. I just can't.

"She's still got a few hours. Come on, I'll make some tea. At least stay until Marcel gets back. You don't want to leave me alone on Christmas Eve, do you, Blake?"

Heidi knows me too well. No. I'd never leave her alone. Enough people in her life have left her. I would dearly love to choke my best friend out, though. Where the fuck is he?

At least he'd be a good distraction from being alone with Heidi. I wouldn't be having all these filthy thoughts in my filthy fucking head if her brother was here with us.

Footsteps thunder up the front porch steps.

Thank fuck.

Heidi throws open the door. "Axel! What are you doing here?"

Oh, fuck no.

"You're freezing! Come in, come in," Heidi squeals.

You've gotta be fuckin' kidding me.

Who's this punk?

He grins down at Heidi. "I didn't wanna interrupt you, if you're doing family stuff, but I wanted to give you this. I'm going out of town with my folks tomorrow."

Folks? Who is this asshole?

The little shit flicks his gaze in my direction. His eyes widen in surprise. That's right, take a good look, motherfucker. I pull my shoulders back and bump my fists together to drive home my irritation at his intrusion.

Heidi flushes and rushes to explain my presence, which seriously pisses me off. "Axel, this is my brother's friend...my friend too, Blake. Blake, this is a friend of mine from school—Axel."

We shake hands and I just barely restrain myself from doing the obvious thing—trying to crush his girly little fingers.

"You go to school with Bug?"

He frowns and glances at Heidi. "Yeah, I graduate this year." He nods at my cut. "You in her brother's MC?"

"Yes." Gee, he can read. Good for him. "You ride?"

He nods and looks me in the eye. Fearless little fuck. "I'm in the process of restoring a '53 Indian Chief."

Interesting project for a kid his age. Almost makes me dislike him a little less.

"It's gonna be really sweet when he's done, Blake, you should see it," Heidi says, making me wonder just how often these two hang out together. Then she does the worst thing. Clapping her hands together, she bounces up and down on her toes, her lovely underage tits bouncing right along.

God help me.

"Oh! Blake, you and Uncle Rock could help him fix it up!" she practically yells, like it's the greatest idea ever.

It's not.

Axel is smarter than I want to give him credit for, because he slowly shakes his head. "That's okay, Heidi." He glances at me again. Guess he'd like me to leave them alone. Tough shit. Hooking my thumbs in my front pockets I adopt a nice, casual pose that says I ain't going anywhere.

"Anyway, I can't stay long, but here." He shoves a big, shiny package at her.

"Oh! It's so heavy. Can I open it now?"

A slow grin spreads over Axel's face. He seems awfully fucking charmed by my little Bug. "Yeah, of course," he answers.

She squeals and rips the paper to shreds, letting it fall all over the floor. It's a book. A big, heavy, text book looking book. What kind of douche gives a girl he's into a fuckin' book?

"Oh my God! Axel, this is so cool!"

The little fuck grins. "It's the same one they use at Hudson Valley, so you know, you can have a head start on everyone."

Tears. Actual fuckin' tears glitter in Heidi's eyes and I want to gut this kid, but I don't know why.

"Thank you so much. This is really awesome. Now I've got something to read over winter break." She glances at him shyly, then at me. Well fuck, I guess she'd like me to get lost.

Too bad.

"Umm. Let me grab my coat so I can walk you out, Axel."

Brushing past me, Heidi sets the book down on

her grandmother's coffee table, then yanks her coat from the rack behind the door.

"I'll be right back, Blake."

She takes Axel's hand and leads him outside.

I'm left with two shitty options. I can follow them out like some creep. Or I can stay inside and watch them through the window like an even bigger creep.

Since it's twenty degrees out, I assume they'll keep their clothes on, so I flip the outside light on for them and head into the living room.

Glancing at the book Axel brought, I'm even more confused. Anatomy and Physiology? What the fuck?

CHAPTER THREE

HEIDI

"Thanks so much, Axel."

"No problem. You okay, Heidi?"

I shrug. "Yeah."

My stomach is flipping like crazy. Axel and I are friends. We were paired up as lab partners in physics class. That's the only reason our worlds ever intersected. Axel's a senior. I'm a junior, but taking advanced science. I thought that would intimidate a guy like Axel, but it doesn't. He's listened to me yap endlessly about Radiologic Technology, which is what I want to study when I graduate from high school. That's how he knew I'd like the book so much.

Wow.

In talking to Axel, I've learned how much he likes motorcycles and I've been waiting for the right time to introduce him to my brother. Unfortunately he met Blake first. I can't believe how rude Blake was to one of my friends. He's never acted like that before.

But then again, I've never had a *boy* friend before.

Not that Axel is my boyfriend. He's just a friend who happens to be a boy. That's what I meant.

"I feel bad. I don't have anything for you."

Axel grins at me. "That's okay. I'm just glad I got to see you open it."

Ohmygod! He's so sweet! I can't wait to go inside to call Penny and Skye and tell them about this! My best friends think it's stupid to take Physics, but they're just jealous of all the time I get to spend with Axel.

I hate that he has to leave so soon. "Are you doing anything fun for Christmas?"

He shrugs. "We're going to visit my older sister. Her husband just split and she needs some help with the kids and stuff."

"I didn't realize you're an uncle?"

"Yup," he answers with a lot of pride in his

voice. "Got a niece and nephew. They're a handful, though. Don't know how she does it."

I want to stay out here talking to him longer. All night really. I love talking to Axel. But it's freezing and I'm pretty sure Blake will flip out if I get in Axel's car, even if it's only to talk.

"Can I call you when I get back?" he asks suddenly.

"Yeah. Of course."

"Cool, maybe we can see a movie or something?" he asks the question casually, but his eyes drill into me, waiting for my answer.

"I'd like that."

He tips his head toward the house. "So, Blake's just a—"

"Family friend," I answer quickly. "I've known him my whole life."

Axel steps a little closer. His hand reaches out and runs over my hair and I almost faint.

Next thing I know, he's leaning in close, brushing his lips over my mine, in a soft feathery kiss.

I'm not cold any more.

No way. I'm burning up.

Axel's hand moves from my hair to the back of my neck as he leans in closer, kissing me harder.

His tongue brushes my bottom lip, which makes me gasp. Then he slips inside, licking and tasting. My hands grip his coat, clutching him closer. I want to press every inch of myself against him, but he's holding himself back.

He pulls away, searching my face. I think he's worried he did something wrong. I don't want him to worry. I want him to kiss me some more.

Fisting my hands in his coat, I tug him close again. I want to reassure him that I liked his kiss, and that I want more. But I don't know what words to use, so I reach up and kiss him. My hands leave his coat and land on the sides of his face, holding him. He responds immediately, stroking his tongue against mine. His hands cup my face, brushing his thumb along my jaw. Oh my God. I want to kiss and lick every inch of him. I want…I want…I don't know what I want because I've never felt this before. I've imagined it. Fantasized about it. But never.

Oh. My. God.

We're both breathless when he pulls away. It's so cold our breath hangs in the air. Heat rises between us.

"Heidi? I…don't want to mess up being friends, but I've wanted to do that for a long time."

Wow.

My skin tingles. Not from the cold. From his words and the sound of his voice. So sincere, with an edge of roughness. My heart feels like it will burst.

"Me too," I answer, while looking at the snow under our feet.

His fingers settle under my chin, tipping my head up. "We'll talk when I get back?"

"Yeah. Definitely."

He starts walking toward his car, but he looks like he's having trouble leaving. I know the feeling because I don't want him to go.

"It's gonna be crazy…with my family and all… but I'll try to call you?"

"Okay."

He opens his car door, then slams it shut and jogs over to me. This time he drops a soft, sweet kiss on my lips.

"Merry Christmas, Heidi."

Murphy

HEIDI'S GOT me pacing the living room like a lunatic. What the fuck is taking them so long?

Good bye Axel. Get lost.

It's not that hard.

Even though I swore up and down I wouldn't, I take a peek out the window, and wish to fuck I hadn't. It's dark. But not so dark I can't see the awestruck expression on Heidi's face as she skips back up the sidewalk. Something happened.

Thank fuck I didn't see whatever it was.

I open the door before she even sets foot on the porch, and watch Axel drive away. Heidi turns and waves.

Christ.

"Everything okay, Bug?"

"Yes," she answers with a dreamy tone that I'd find charming if I didn't suspect that horny dickwad was the cause of it.

She slides off her coat and absently bends over to pick up the wrapping paper she'd dropped earlier.

Stop staring at her ass, motherfucker. She's sixteen.

I glance at the ceiling, because if I try to walk past her and any part of me comes into contact with any part of her, something bad will happen.

"Blake?"

Shifting my focus from the ceiling to Heidi, I find her staring at me.

I jerk my thumb in the direction of the front door. "So, he your boyfriend?"

She shakes her head. "No."

I follow her into the living room, where she stops to touch her book.

"Anatomy and Physiology? Kinda nerdy gift, isn't it?"

Heidi stares up at me with wide eyes. "Yeah, but he knew I wanted it."

I want to ask her how he knew something that seems so personal, but I don't know how to say it in a way that won't make me sound like a jealous dick. I've known Heidi her whole life and it would never occur to me that a big ol' textbook would be something she'd want as a gift.

"Why?"

She cocks her head at me. "You'll think it's dumb."

"No I won't. Tell me."

"Well, I want to go to school to be a radiographer, and that's one of the first classes you have to take. So, I mentioned I'd love to get my hands on one of the textbooks." She glances down at it again and shrugs.

That was a lot of information for me to take in. The last I knew she wanted to be a fashion designer.

"What the heck is a radiographer? I thought you wanted to be a fashion designer?"

Her face twists.

I mime an imitation of sewing in the air with my hands. "I remember you used to sew all those little dresses and—"

"Ugh. For my Barbies, when I was like, ten, Blake!" she yells, stomping her foot.

I'm used to her dramatic little outbursts, so it comes naturally to ignore the whole stomping her feet thing. "So what? You were good at it."

"I also wanted to ride a unicorn to school. Geez, Blake. It's a medical job. Taking x-rays and stuff. But I can be done in two years and make good money when I finish."

"Why not just go to med school then?"

"Because it takes too long and costs a fortune."

"Bug, you know between your brother and me you can go wherever you want? You know that, right?"

Her face softens a little. "I know and I appreciate that. Honestly though, I don't think I could hack all the years of med school. This seems manageable and there are a lot of jobs to be had when I'm done."

"Well, sounds smart then."

Fuck, she impresses me. Heidi could sit on her ass and do nothing if she wanted to and we'd take care of her. In fact I always assumed…Well it doesn't matter what I thought. She wants to make her own way. I respect that.

"So, how come you never told me this before?"

She shrugs. "We don't talk the way we used to."

Now I feel like shit. Between my responsibilities with the club running me ragged and me trying to avoid getting into an inappropriate situation with Heidi, she's right. I've been avoiding her.

"I'm sorry. You can always call me, you know."

"Yeah. I don't want to be a bother, though."

Aw fuck. That's probably my doing. "You never bother me."

She snorts because how many times in her life have I teased her by saying she's a pain in my ass?

"So, you like this Axel guy?"

A shy smile passes her lips. "Yeah. He's fun to talk to. He's my physics lab partner."

Something painful shifts in my chest, but I reach out and ruffle her hair to distract myself. "Good. That mean you're not crushin' on me anymore?"

Heidi pushes her lips into a pout. Six years ago, that face annoyed the crap out of me. Mostly because it made me give into whatever demands she was making at the time. Now, the expression is somehow sexy. And while I know it's not designed to excite me, it does.

Great. Just what I need.

Tears shimmer in her big brown eyes, digging the stab of guilt I already feel even deeper.

"Sorry to tell you, but I've been over that for a while now, Blake."

Well, fuck if that doesn't knock the breath out of me.

When I don't respond—because I have no fucking idea what to say to that—she spins away, storming into the kitchen.

The sound of pots and pans banging around reaches me all the way out here, so I decide I better go fix this shitty situation I just caused.

Her back is to me when I walk in the kitchen and her shoulders clearly shaking.

"Heidi, I'm sorry."

"You know how many times I've seen you with those skanks that hang out up at your club?"

"Heidi—"

"Or when I walked in on you and—"

"Heidi!" Fuck, I don't need the reminder of that clusterfuckin' nightmare.

She turns, but she's not crying. She's pissed.

There's something about a beautiful, pissed-off woman, that's always excited me.

Girl. Sixteen-year-old girl. Not woman.

Fuck!

"You've been pushing me away for years. And now you're gonna act jealous 'cause I like a guy I go to school with?"

For a kid, she's got me pegged a little too well.

Frustrated, I rake my fingers through my hair. Christ, she makes me want to rip it out in fistfuls. "Fuck, Heidi! You're sixteen. I'm eight god damn years older than you. Your brother is my best fuckin' friend. What do you want from me?"

Heidi's never been one to hide her feelings, so she yells right back at me. "You didn't have to be so mean. You didn't have to hurt—never mind."

"What'd you want me to do, *wait for you*, sweetheart?"

Her eyes narrow at my sarcastic tone, and in that moment I really hate myself.

"No, Blake. Not at all. But don't be surprised if I don't wait for you either."

Like fucking hell.

"Bug!" Someone shouts from the front of the house.

Great, *now* Teller shows up.

Teller's boots thud over the hardwood floors. "Murph, you here too?"

"Yeah, man."

Heidi turns away from me, leaning over the sink to splash water on her face.

Teller enters the kitchen all smiles. "Where ya been, fucker?" I grumble at him.

Perceptive as always, he glances at Heidi, then at me. "Everything okay here?"

"Yeah man, we're cool."

"Hey Marcel." Heidi turns and launches herself at her big brother, who wraps her in his arms, picking her up and spinning her the way he's done forever.

"How ya doin'? Lights outside look real pretty, baby sis."

"Thanks. Blake helped me put them up."

Teller glances at me over his shoulder. "Thanks, Bro."

"No problem. You missed it, Heidi's boyfriend stopped by."

I chuckle watching the grin fall from Teller's face as he holds her out at arm's length. "What boyfriend?"

Heidi glares at me. "Shut up, Blake. He's just a friend from school."

"He brought her a present too," I tattle like a little bitch. But at least I can breathe again. This is familiar territory. Comfortable, teasing, appropriate territory.

Heidi keeps up her mean-girl stare and I can't help chuckling.

Teller quirks an eyebrow at her. "Oh yeah?"

"Yes. A book. He's a nice guy. We're probably going to go to a movie when he gets back from his family's."

We'll see about that.

"Gram meet him?"

"No."

Teller nods. "Let me know, I want to meet the kid. Scare the shit out of him, so he knows not to mess with you."

"Fuck off. Blake already acted like a dick to him."

Teller and I both laugh, which infuriates Heidi. She storms off into the living room.

"Marcel!" she yelps.

Worried, I take off to find her staring at one big-ass green tree in the living room, with a lot of other boxes and bags around it.

"Gram's gonna shit herself when she sees this," Heidi says with a smile.

"Yeah, I know, but you should have a tree. She can take it up with me. I'll clean it up after New Year's."

Heidi

As much as I'd like to, I'm never able to stay mad at Blake for long. He doesn't mention Axel again. He and my brother spend time bullshitting. Like they don't spend enough time at the clubhouse doing that.

But whatever, I'm just happy to be around them. I miss my big brother. At ten years older than me, he's not old enough to be a father figure, but he's the closest I've ever had to one. He and Grams don't get along anymore, so he doesn't come around as much, and I hate it. Although he does make sure to take me out to lunch every Friday when I get dismissed from school early. I look forward to it all week long.

We finish decorating the tree and it looks pretty nice for a rush job.

Since they're not paying attention to me, I slip my cell phone out and send Penny a text.

Axel stopped by with xmas prezzie for me.

Shut up!

We kissed.

Call me!

Can't Bro and Blake are here.

Call later.

Lost in my conversation with Penny, I didn't notice the conversation around me had gone silent. Blake's staring over my shoulder. I quickly shut my phone off and shove it in my pocket.

"Stop being nosy."

His jaw muscles are working, like he's grinding his teeth, but he doesn't say anything.

"Where's Marcel?" I ask because the silence is crawling over my skin in uncomfortable waves.

"He went outside to pay the pizza delivery guy."

Oh wow, I must have really zoned out there for a minute.

"Come get it while it's hot," Marcel shouts from the kitchen.

Blake pats my shoulder. "Hungry?"

"Starved."

He half-smiles at me.

After dinner, Marcel runs up to the attic to rummage around for more decorations.

"I'm takin' off, bro," Blake shouts up the stairs and gets a muffled response from my brother.

Blake turns to me and offers his hand. "Walk me out?"

"Yeah, sure."

The night is beautiful. Cold, crisp and bright. The stars are glittering like diamonds and I almost slip on a small patch of ice because I'm so busy staring up at the sky instead of walking.

"Careful, sweetheart," Blake cautions in a hushed voice, gripping my hand tighter.

When we get to his car, he opens the trunk and pulls out a few boxes.

"What's that?"

"For you."

Suddenly I feel like crying.

Blake sets the packages back down. "What's wrong?"

I let out a sad sniffle. "Nothing."

"Heidi—"

I wave my hand in the air between us. "I'm fine. Just sad. Grams and I—I miss my mom, too, you know?"

"Yeah, I know."

I feel a little bad for yelling at him earlier, when

he gave up his whole night to help me do silly stuff. "Thank you for everything today."

"You're welcome. I'm sorry—" Blake's actually apologizing to me? Now, I feel even worse.

"No. It's okay. I'd rather argue with you than nothing at all," I say with another sniffle.

Blake chuckles. "That's awful."

"I know."

"Come here." He pulls me tight for a hug, and all the craziness pinging around inside of me stills as I relax and breathe the scent of Blake in. "Heidi, I'm trying really hard here," he mumbles against my hair.

I don't even know what that's supposed to mean, so I just hug him tighter. "What?"

He shifts me away from him so we're staring at each other, our noses only inches apart. "I'm trying hard to do the right thing by you." His voice is deep and husky in a way I've never heard before.

"What does that mean?"

"It means, I care about you. You're not like a little sister to me anymore, but I can't do anything about it right now."

Something pulses to life inside of me. Heat races through me, even though I'm freezing. I can't keep my emotions in check any longer. I think I understand what he's trying to tell me. My heart actually hurts. I'm not sure if I believe him or he's just trying to cheer me up.

"I know you don't really mean any of that. I appreciate you trying to—"

He groans as if he's in pain. "Heidi, look at me. Please don't make this harder."

We're only inches apart and I try searching his eyes, but they're the same as they always are, unreadable to me. He doesn't say anything else, but suddenly his mouth is on mine and the electricity that slams though me is so intense, I don't know what to do. A low moan slides out of me, and Blake groans. His hands come up to cup my face, holding me the way he wants. His tongue sweeps in and my hands curl into his coat, pulling him closer. Heat pounds through me, leaving me aching, restless and so confused. He finally tears himself away from me and I let out a startled cry. I wasn't ready to stop.

"We can't. I'm sorry, Heidi. I shouldn't have—"

"Please don't. It's okay. I want—"

Blake hands are fisted at his sides. "It's not okay. Don't you understand? Your brother. Fuck, the club. I can't. We can't. Not now." He runs the back of his hand over my cheek, warming me. "You're so fuckin' pretty, Heidi."

"Really?"

"Yeah, girl. I try not to notice, but it's impossible."

My eyes tear up, but it's so cold, I think the tears are frozen in place.

"Thank you."

"I better go."

"Okay. Are you coming back tomorrow?"

"Probably not."

My heart breaks a little. I have a sick feeling that after tonight, I won't see Blake for a while.

He leans over, grabbing the boxes again. "Here. Go get inside and warm up."

I take the bundle and can barely see over the top.

"Go on. Let me watch you go inside."

"Merry Christmas, Blake."

Murphy

I'M out of my fucking mind.

I kissed Heidi.

Shit.

Christ, if Teller finds out he'll string me up by my fuckin' balls. Then probably hand me over to

Rock and Wrath so they can kick the shit out of me.

That sweet, fuckin' little girl. Thinkin' I don't care about her. That I don't love her. Fuck, that kills me. The hurt, confused look on her face just about did me in. I've got no business messin' with her head like that, and then leaving her alone to deal with all the feelings I stirred up.

Every time I try to do right by her, I fuckin' hurt her.

I refuse to dwell on how sweet she tastes. Even though it's impossible with her scent still clinging to me. I can't think about how right she felt in my arms, because I know it's wrong. I can't think about any of it or I'll lose control and do something even stupider.

No. I'm going straight to Crystal Ball, and beggin' Rock to send me on a long-ass run.

Anywhere away from here. I got eighteen more months of this fuckin' torture to live through before I can claim my girl.

In the back of my head a voice is telling me it will be too late. That's a long fuckin' time at Heidi's age. She's already got that little punk, Axel, sniffin' around her.

My fist slams into the steering wheel. Fuck! I'm

such a dick for messin' with her head, just because I got all jealous. Seeing that text to her friend about Axel kissing her sent burning pain through my chest. Still, I wasn't going to do anything about it. But then I went and put my arms around her, trying to comfort her. And the feel of her against me, her scent…I couldn't help it.

Fuck me. I don't think talking to Rock will be the only thing I do at Crystal Ball tonight. Plenty of the girls will be looking for company on Christmas Eve.

Some fuckin' Christmas.

WRATH & TRINITY

CHAPTER FOUR

WRATH

As I step in the front door of the clubhouse, I'm greeted with the sight of Trinity rummaging around on the floor of the front hall closet. Normally it would be an exciting and rare treat to find Trin on her knees, but she looks so adorably frustrated, I don't have it in me to hassle her tonight.

"Do you need help?"

She jumps, banging her elbow into the door frame.

"Ow, fuck. Why you gotta sneak up on me, Wrath?"

"Shit, I'm sorry."

She's still rubbing her elbow, but her gaze is

focused on the back of the closet. After another wince of pain, she drops her hands to the floor and crawls deeper into the closet. Her ass is covered in dusty grime, but it doesn't dull the lust in me at all. I still want to peel off every frustrating layer of clothing that's keeping her skin hidden.

"Can you grab this?" she asks, holding up a small box without looking at me.

I have no idea what she's up to, but with most of the brothers gone for the holidays, I've got nothing better to do anyway.

Plus, any time I get to spend around Trinity is time well spent. Even if most of the time we end up arguing and being mean to each other. It would be awesome foreplay if she'd actually let me fuck her again. It's been at least three years.

Three very long years.

Besides the awful love/hate thing we got going on between us, I actually find her interesting. There are few females who actually interest me.

Trinity is unlike any other woman I've ever known. Her unique blend of bitchy and fragile has fascinated me since the night we met almost seven years ago. She's not quite the same girl I remember. The vulnerability that first drew me to her is still there, but it's different. Now she's also more relaxed, more confident. She jokes around and even teases us sometimes.

Every single one of my MC brothers would protect her with their life. Especially me. Even though she pisses me off something fierce most of the time.

"What's in the box?" I ask. More to have something to say than out of curiosity.

"Ornaments."

Well, now I'm curious.

"What are you going to do with them? We don't have a tree in the clubhouse."

She points behind the bar. "Yes, I do. Z brought me one before he took off. It's one of those potted pines. He's going to plant it for me in the spring."

Huh.

Z bought her fucking Christmas tree. Don't I feel like a dick? I've never given her a damn thing. Except my cock and a lot of grief.

Brushing off her hands, she stands and pushes past me. Even that brief bit of contact stirs me. Ducking behind the bar, she pulls out the tree. It's a tiny little thing.

"Looks like Charlie Brown's fuckin' tree," I tell her.

She squints at me. "I can't believe you've seen that."

"What? A Charlie Brown Christmas? Doesn't every kid watch it growing up?"

A small smile plays over her lips. "It's just funny thinking of you as a kid."

"Why? Aren't I pretty much a big, overgrown kid, now?"

That makes her laugh. Full force, genuine laughter. No fake shit from Trinity.

"Yup," she finally answers.

TRINITY

It's nice joking around with Wrath for a change. Under normal circumstances we would probably ignore each other or try to make each other jealous in some unsavory way. I'm not proud of it, but that's what our relationship boils down to these days.

He helps me unwrap the little ornaments I keep stashed away. Nothing special, but they make me happy.

"Oh, hang on. Rock got me these little strands of Christmas lights, let me grab those before we start sticking the ornaments on."

Wrath gives me a strange look, but doesn't say anything as I dash down the hall to my room. There's a bag with an extra tiny strand of lights and small ropes of gold garland that Rock dropped off at my door before leaving to manage the MC's strip club, Crystal Ball, today. At the time I had no idea what he expected me to decorate with them. Unusually flustered, Rock mumbled something about waiting for Z and took off.

Of course when Z stopped by with the little potted tree, it all made more sense.

I feel like I'm missing something, but glancing around my room doesn't give me any idea what it is, so I shut the door behind me and walk back to the living room.

Wrath's busy unwrapping ornaments for me and setting them out in neat little rows. He's so precise it makes me laugh.

He glances at me with a lop-sided grin. "What?"

I gesture at the rows of ornaments and he shrugs. "I never knew you were so anal."

He wiggles his eyebrows at me. "I can be if you'd like."

"Jerk." I give him a playful punch in the arm, which honestly probably hurt me more than him. His arms are like granite.

He taps the bar top with his finger. "Some of these are way too big for that little tree."

"I know."

We decorate the tree in no time. When we get the last strand of garland wrapped around it, Wrath lifts his head. For a second I almost get lost in his ocean blue eyes that I used to love so much.

"Are you cooking something?"

"Oh my god!" I jump up and race down to the kitchen. Wrath's heavy footsteps pound down the hall after me, but I'm more focused on getting to the oven in time. I'd forgotten all about the cookies!

CHAPTER FIVE

WRATH

WHAT THE HELL?

One minute we're sitting here havin' a moment, decoratin' her tree, the next she's off and running down the hall like a scalded cat.

"Trin, you okay?"

The scent of burned cookies reaches my nose and I gag.

I flip on the oven fan and open the back door to clear the room.

"Dammit!" Poor Trin looks like she's going to cry.

Rushing over, I grab the tray of ruined cookies out of her hand without thinking. The metal sears my fingers. "Fuck! That's hot." The tray goes flying on the counter as I shake off the sting.

Her honey eyes sparkle with amusement. "Duh, it just came out of the oven." Trin waves her oven mitts in my face.

While I'm running my hand under some cold water I ask her if she's okay.

"Yeah, my cookies are ruined though."

A glance at the little black lumps confirms this. "Yeah, no saving those. Can you make more?"

"I can. They're just a pain in the ass. I still have half a batch of dough for them though. Rock and I are the only ones who eat them, so it's not a big deal."

My face scrunches up. I hate those little ginger cookies, she and Rock love so much. Fucking ginger has no business being in baked goods.

"What else you making this year?"

I know she makes her regular cookies and one new one every year, so I'm curious to know what the new one is.

She grins. "Brownie cookies are the new ones this year."

"Sounds like a chick thing."

"Good, then you don't get any."

"Oh, you'll give me your cookies, or else, little girl," I tease her in an especially low, pervy voice.

She giggles, her burned cookies forgotten. "You sound so creepy."

"That's what I was goin' for, baby."

Still laughing, she shakes her head at me, and reaches for an apron. For the first time today, I take in the entire room. She's got four neat little stations set up in our large, industrial-sized kitchen.

She follows my gaze around the room. "I need another oven," she says.

"You got two."

"Yeah, and like eleven bikers to bake cookies for."

Something about the way she says that strikes me funny.

"Stop laughing at me."

"I'm not Trin. Swear."

Messing with Trinity when she's in the cooking zone is never a good idea. She hates it when any of us touch stuff in her kitchen. Especially when she's in the middle of a project.

I pull out a beer, sit at the kitchen table, and watch her work instead.

"You mind if I open another window, babe? It's hotter than hell in here."

"Yeah, sure."

When I turn around I have to stifle a groan. She's stripped off her sweatshirt and is left standing there in a skimpy tank top and flannel pants. Like most girls, she's got an elastic stashed in her somewhere on her body, and she gathers up all her pretty gold hair, tying it up in a messy knot on top of her head.

Fuck, she's cute.

"Do you want some Christmas punch?"

"No thanks, babe." That stuff she makes is so sweet, it makes my teeth sweat thinking about it.

It seems like hours go by as I watch her work.

"You don't have to stay here, Wrath. I'm fine. There's got to be someplace else you'd rather be on Christmas Eve."

The truth is, there isn't anywhere else I want to be. But I don't know how to say that to her after all the shit we've done to each other.

When I don't answer, she throws a glance at me over her shoulder. "Don't want to hang at Crystal Ball with Rock?"

"Fuck no. Nothing more depressing than a strip club on Christmas Eve."

"Poor Rock, I'm sure he's having a rough night."

Inside I'm laughing my ass off. Rock thinks none of us know he's stopped nailing his regular stable of girls while he's pining away for his hot lawyer chick.

"What do you know about it?"

Trinity snickers. "You think the girls aren't talking about that all the time? Cookie's lost her fuckin' mind over it."

"Christ, don't we have some rule around this place that says no gossiping about the guys?"

She snorts. "Good luck with that."

By the time she's done with her baking, she's flushed and sweaty all over. I approach her with the intention of helping her clean up the mess she's made. Except she's walking backwards from the oven and bumps right into me. I cup my hands over her shoulders to steady her. Out of nowhere it hits me that my hands are touching her bare, warm skin.

Without even thinking about it, I lean down and press my lips to her neck. Fuck, she smells good. Spices, sugar, and something else unique to Trinity.

My hand slides into her hair, tugging it free from the elastic. All her soft, golden waves fall down around her shoulders.

"Wyatt," she whispers and my eyes pop open at

her tone. She's still holding a tray of cookies in her trembling hands.

"Set the tray down, Trin." I growl the words in her ear and almost lose it when she shivers against me.

She sets the tray down.

"Are you all done out here?" I whisper in her ear.

My cheek brushes against hers and she's burning up. Not surprising since she's been in front of the ovens for hours, but I'm still concerned. Grabbing her chin, I turn her face toward me. She's all flushed, but not in the way I'd been hoping for. Pressing the back of my hand over her forehead, I also notice how glassy her eyes are.

"Trin, you okay?"

She answers in a shaky voice. "I don't feel so good, Wyatt."

My gaze skips to the pitcher of Christmas punch. "How much did you have to drink?"

"I dunno," she answers weakly.

All of a sudden she jerks out of my grasp and rushes to the sink. Hands curled over the lip she leans over and retches.

"Shit, babe." I feel so fucking useless, standing there, holding her hair, rubbing my hand in circles over her back. I'd do anything to stop the violent spasms taking hold of her body.

After an eternity, she stops puking, runs some cold water over her wrists and splashes her face. A miserable groan drifts out of her.

"You okay, baby?"

"I don't know. I'm so sorry."

"For what?"

Instead of answering, she turns away and starts spewing again.

"Honey, you think I should take you to the hospital?"

"No," she groans. "You don't have to stick around. I'm gross."

Like fuck am I gonna leave her alone when she's this sick.

"Babe, it's fine."

"I'm sorry."

"Stop sayin' you're sorry. I mean, I know we don't always get along, but puking your guts out just 'cause I kissed you, seems a little extreme, don't you think?"

She lets out a soft chuckle and I can't even describe how grateful I am to hear it.

"Can you help me out to the living room?"

"Don't you think you should go to bed?"

"No. I'd rather sleep out on the couch if I'm sick."

"Okay. Hold on. Try not to barf on me."

As gentle as possible, I swing her up into my arms and carry her down the hall to the living room. I drop her on the couch without jarring her too much.

Her teeth are clicking together like crazy. "I'm so cold."

"Give me a second." It takes a few minutes, but I locate a bunch of clean blankets and get a fire going in the fireplace. After I get her all bundled up, she snuggles into the blankets and sighs.

"Better?"

"Mmmhmm."

Just in case, I set a bucket on the floor next to her. Before settling in next to her, I bring her little tree over and set it on the coffee table, so she'll see it when she wakes up.

CHAPTER SIX

TRINITY

UGH. I wanna die.

I can't remember the last time I felt this awful.

While I don't have a high tolerance for alcohol, it's never made me this sick. I'm guessing I caught the flu or something. I hate being sick. I hate puking.

I really hate being weak in front of anyone.

Especially Wrath. I'm burning up. Not only from fever but from humiliation.

Slowly I slide my foot down the couch and my toe connects with something solid.

"Wyatt?"

He seems to startle awake with a sharp intake of breath.

"What do you need? You okay?"

"My tummy hurts."

"There's a bucket if you think you're gonna be sick."

Reaching out from under the blanket, my hand flaps around in the air until it connects with the bucket.

"Thanks."

"Think you can keep some water down? I don't want you to get dehydrated."

I groan at the thought. I never want to eat or drink anything again.

"You don't have to stay with me. I'm okay."

He snorts. "I ain't leaving you alone like this. Go back to sleep."

"Okay."

Eventually I drift off.

WRATH

Around midnight, Teller steps in the front door. Before he can open his loud mouth, I slash my hand through the air, motioning for him to be quiet.

"What's up?" he whispers.

"She's sick."

"Aw, fuck. She said she didn't feel well this morning."

Setting aside my jealousy, I curl my finger at him to come closer.

"Can you sit with her? I'm gonna clean up the kitchen. She had just finished baking all her cookies when she got sick."

"Yeah, sure. Bring me back a cookie."

I mutter a "fuck you" at him and he laughs.

Teller takes my place on the couch and even though I don't want to leave, I do. 'Cause if I know Trinity, sick or not, she'll be up tomorrow fixing up the kitchen.

When I'm done with the clean up, I poke around in the fridge. Annoyed I can't find what I want, I slam the door.

Teller's still awake, staring at the tree when I walk back into the living room.

He tips his chin up at the tree. "You get that for her?"

"Nah. Z did. Rock got her those little lights."

He just nods in return. "That's cool."

"How's Bug?"

A grin lights up my friend's face. He loves that lil' brat something fierce. "She's good. Got some boy from school sniffin' around her. Murphy all but pissed around the house to scare him away."

I gotta slap my hand over my mouth, so I don't bark out a laugh that wakes Trin up. "Nice."

I'm so tense and fidgety, I can't sit still. "I'm gonna run out and get some ginger ale or somethin' for her. She'll get dehydrated and feel ten times worse if she doesn't drink something. You'll sit with her?"

"Yeah, no problem. You want me to run out and grab stuff? Not much will be open. You'll have to go all the way down into Empire."

"Nah, it's fine."

MY FIRST STOP is Crystal Ball. I find Rock sitting at the bar watching the door, looking miserable as fuck.

"What up, prez?"

He gives me a weary smile. CB is depressing as hell tonight. At least to me it is. But the girls have decorated the fuck out of everything and that's what I'm here for.

I slide onto the stool next to him and signal Willow to bring me a bottle of water.

Rock, as always, is no bullshit. "I know you didn't come here for a lap dance, so what's up?"

"Trin's not feeling well. Ran out to get a few things for her. Just thought I'd see if you needed any help here."

He raises an eyebrow at me. "She okay?"

"Yeah. Teller's sittin' with her. Everything all right here?"

He shrugs. "Girls say they're makin' bank. No one's started any trouble. So, I guess."

"You coulda made one of the other guys deal with this."

He waves his hand in the air, dismissing my suggestion. "Nah. The guys that got families to go home to should do that. I'm fine."

It's suicide to ask my next question, but I do it anyway. I'm kinda stupid that way. "You talk to Hope yet?"

Rock glares at me.

"First holiday without her husband. Probably rough on her."

More glaring.

"How long you gonna wait?"

His jaw twitches. "Couple more months."

I nod. Really, I just want him to get this bitch out of his system. I hate seeing my best friend so twisted over some civilian woman who'll probably make his life miserable.

Giving him a hearty slap on the back, I slide off my stool and head toward his office.

Bingo.

The girls weren't very subtle. There's mistletoe up over Rock's door. And strung up along the hallway outside his office.

A big, blinking neon sign would have been less obvious.

I don't think Rock will mind if I borrow the decorations. In fact, I think he'll be relieved.

"Hey, Wrath. What ya think you're doin'?"

"Hey Lex. Borrowing some mistletoe."

"We put it up for Rock."

"Yeah, well, I don't think he appreciates it this year."

"Do you know what's going on with him? He's barely ever here any more."

I do, but it's none of her business. "No, just leave him alone."

"Okay. So, what are *you* doing tonight?"

I glance over at Lexi. The invitation in her voice was clear enough. But in case I missed it, she's standing there in a "let's fuck pose" that would normally do the trick. No doubt she's a sexy girl, but I got other things on my mind tonight.

"Family stuff," I answer, hoping she'll get lost.

"I brought those decorations in, you know." Her tone makes it clear what she's after. These fuckin' dancers are all the same.

Flipping out my wallet, I hand her two twenties. "Will that cover it?"

She stuffs the bills into her tiny little g string and smiles at me. "Sure, thanks."

"Later, Lexi."

I salute Rock on my way out the door.

My next stop is the pharmacy. Gotta love these big-box ones that are open twenty-four hours, three-sixty-five. The pharmacist behind the counter doesn't look old enough to shave yet, but he gives me a list of stuff that he thinks should make Trin feel better based on the info I give him.

Teller's still awake when I get back to the clubhouse.

"She wake up?" I whisper as I get closer.

"No. Been moaning and thrashing around a lot though."

I'm torn. I want to wake her and get some fluids

in her—no, not that kind—but I also want her to rest.

"You can go."

Teller cocks his head at me, but gets up and leaves us alone.

CHAPTER SEVEN

TRINITY

IN MY BARFY HAZE, I'm aware of someone getting up and leaving the room. Then the couch dips and by the sigh, I know it's Wrath.

My mouth is so dry I can barely talk. "Did you go somewhere?" I croak out the words, my throat so raw it hurts to talk.

"Did we wake you up?" he asks.

"No."

"How do you feel?"

"Gross."

He chuckles softly, then sits up. The rustling of a plastic bag, fizz of a bottle opening, paper ripping.

None of the sounds are compelling enough for me to open my eyes.

"Think you can drink something for me?" Wrath asks.

At his request, I sit up and instantly regret it. Pain slices through my head, and I fall back with a moan.

"You're getting dehydrated. Here, drink some of this."

He nudges a bottle in my hand. Even stuck a straw in it for me. I sip at the ginger ale thinking nothing has ever tasted so good.

"Want some crackers?"

"Ugh. One thing at a time."

He takes the soda from my hand and sets it on the table.

"You move my tree?" I ask after a minute.

"Yeah."

"Thanks."

I poke at him with my toes and he grabs my feet, settling them in his lap, warming them with his big hands.

"You don't have to stay down here with me."

He doesn't answer right away. "You had me worried."

"Sorry. I hope you don't end up catching whatever it is."

"I'm not worried about that."

"You should be, I feel like I got hit by a bus."

"Try to rest now, babe."

I turn over and manage to fall asleep.

I wake to sunlight pouring in the living room. Wrath's sprawled out on the other couch sound asleep. Everything aches, but at least my stomach seems calmer. Probably 'cause there's nothing left in it. My head's pounding, so I swipe the half empty bottle of ginger ale off the table and suck some of it down.

Now that the worst is over, I need to crawl into my own bed. I feel bad leaving Wrath out here alone, after he took such good care of me, but I think he'll understand. I drape one of the blankets over him and he doesn't stir. It blows my mind that he was up all night taking care of me. I want to lean over and kiss his cheek, but I'm afraid of waking him. At least that's what I tell myself.

Even sick, I have to stop and admire him. In sleep, he looks almost angelic. You'd never guess what a scary jerk he can be when he's awake. It's nice to see this side of him again.

It's been awhile.

WRATH

Naturally, Trinity's gone when I wake up.

She took the bag of stuff I brought her, though, so that's good.

Still, I'd like to know if she's okay.

As I wander down the hall, I wonder if she noticed the mistletoe I left for her.

Probably not.

I hesitate before knocking, because I shouldn't be waking her up. Then I hear her shower running.

Now I'm thinking about her naked.

Great.

When the shower turns off, I finally knock.

She answers in flannel pajamas and a towel on her head.

Her skin is still sickly pale, and she's got deep circles under her eyes. She's still so stinkin' cute.

"You okay?"

"Meh. I don't feel like puking any more. But I still feel like shit. Thanks for the stuff you got for me, I know it was probably a pain in the ass to find someplace open…"

"Trin, it's no big deal."

"I'll get breakfast—"

"No you won't. You're going to rest. Your only

options today are couch or your bedroom." My bedroom would also be a fine choice, but I leave it out. "I catch you in the kitchen, I'm gonna spank your ass."

Her eyes widen, shocked. I'm a little shocked myself. Because I actually mean it.

"Take a sick day, Trin. We'll survive."

She nods.

I point to the mistletoe hanging in her doorway. "Look up."

A soft giggle that gets me thinking all sorts of inappropriate things comes out of her.

"Do you really think that's a good idea?"

I hate what she's implying and it's on the tip of my tongue to respond with something nasty. But I really don't want to fight with Trinity today.

Instead, I lean over and kiss her forehead.

"Merry Christmas. Now get some rest."

ZERO & LILLY

CHAPTER EIGHT

ZERO

I SHOULDN'T BE GOING to visit Lilly.

Not tonight.

Not on Christmas Eve.

I know she comes from a big, tight-knit Russian family, so she's probably not even home.

It's fuckin' stupid for me to drive all the way up to see her. Especially if I just want to get laid.

I can do that back at the clubhouse.

Until half an hour ago I'd been at my own awkward family dinner. My blood family, not the MC. It's tricky business navigating the minefield of family relations around the holidays. Eventually people drink too much and start listing all the ways you've disappointed them with the way you're living your life. I managed to stay until a physical unease built up so strong, it pushed me out the door.

Way too fucking cold to ride my bike, I'm trapped in my black truck, racing up the Northway.

To see a girl who may not want to see me. Who fuck, may not even be home. Or even worse, if she *is* home, may have some other guy over.

I do *not* like that idea.

At all.

I blame Rock for my predicament. My MC president and one of my best friends. I'd never have met Lilly if he wasn't so damn obsessed with Lilly's friend—his former lawyer—Hope. Sweet as they come, Hope is the last woman you'd expect to find dating an MC prez. Sometimes it shocks me she's managed to stay friends with Lilly for so long. All class and beauty on the outside, with the foulest mouth and an appetite for sex to match any man, Lilly keeps me on my toes.

She doesn't care if I fuck around with other chicks, because she's fucking other guys.

First time this scenario has ever annoyed me.

Tonight I didn't bother calling first. Last time I went that route, she told me she was busy. I'm not giving her an out tonight.

I even have a present with me.

No, not my dick. That comes later.

Her driveway is dark, but that's not unusual. Christ, I feel like a stalky dickwad. Her porch light is on, but her little Lexus sedan is nowhere to be seen.

Fuck.

I knew it was a risk coming all the way up here.

I'm still douching around in her driveway, trying to decide if I should wait or head back down to Empire, when headlights come bouncing down the driveway. I swear my dick pulses to life at the sight.

CHAPTER NINE

LILLY

I MANAGED to bite back the tears until I got in my car. Over the years I've learned nothing can pierce your heart more than family. At thirty-three, it is scandalous that I'm not married and carting a bunch of kids around with me. Never mind that I paid for college and graduate school all by myself. That I bought my own house before I turned thirty with my own money. That I haven't asked my parents for a dime since I left home at eighteen.

If it wasn't for my older brother, Alex, playing mediator, I wouldn't have lasted through my mother's mushroom soup with *zaprashka*—the first of twelve miserable courses I sat through tonight.

Even though my mother bent her traditions a long time ago, and now celebrates Christmas Eve on the 24th of December instead of January 7th, the meal she makes has not changed.

How badly I wanted to take comfort in the familiar smells and tastes of my childhood. But once my mother got busy picking out my flaws and failures, it was only a matter of time before my father, aunts, and cousins joined the fun.

Lilly, when you gonna find a man to take care of you?

I can take care of myself, Babbo.

Nonsense, you're getting too old to attract a man.

Zia Bruna, I attract plenty of men.

That one had not gone over well. I'm pretty sure my family still thinks I'm a virgin.

I hate to break it to them, but that ship sailed a long time ago.

Why hadn't I moved farther away?

I could call my best friend, Sophie. Before her parents divorced, their strict Greek expectations of her rivaled my own family's. But she's off in New Hampshire spending the holiday with her rock star boyfriend who has some downtime until after New Year's.

After a quick stop at Stewart's, I have a quart of my favorite eggnog in my possession. When I get home, I'm going to introduce the eggnog to the bottle of Bailey's Irish Cream I have stashed in my fridge. Then I'm going to crawl into bed and forget that I have to get up and do this again tomorrow.

My heart jumps in my throat at the sight of a black SUV parked near my house. Nestled at the end of a long, bumpy driveway, my house is isolated—which is how I've always liked it. My foot slips off the accelerator as I process what I want to do. Turn around and drive away? Call 911? Call Alex?

Before I can do any of those things, the door swings open and a big, black-booted foot steps out. Z.

My mouth quirks. I swear to God, my nipples tighten and a slick rush of heat dampens my panties.

Christmas Eve just got a whole lot better.

CHAPTER TEN

ZERO

"Z? What are you doing here?"

Her throaty voice gets me so fucking hard, my dick's banging against my zipper.

Showtime.

Snagging the package off the front seat, I meet her in the driveway.

"Wanted to give you your Christmas present."

She cocks her head in a way I don't find all that comforting. But her hand reaches out to take the bag. Before her fingers skim over the brown paper sack, I yank it away.

"Nu-uh. Not yet."

She plants a fist on her hip and gives me a cool

stare that's hot as fuck. "You don't have to bring me presents if you want to get laid. You and your big cock are enough."

Raising my hand and flattening my palm over my heart, I answer her in a wounded voice. "What a sweet-talker. Now, are you gonna invite me in? It's so fuckin' cold I can see your nipples through your wool coat."

Her mouth twitches with a repressed grin. I'm gettin' to her. Next thing I know, she's standing flush against me, pushing me back in small steps until my back is against my car.

"Not so fast, sexy girl." Slapping the bag on the roof, I flip places and pin her up against my car. Her mouth forms a small "o" of surprise, but I take it in a rough kiss before she gets out a sound.

Then her hands are in my hair, pulling me closer. My arms snake around her waist, holding her tight to me.

Fuck, I've missed this. No one tastes like Lilly. Smells like her. Feels like her.

So fucking good.

Breathlessly, she pulls away.

"Do you want to come inside?"

Hell, fucking, yes.

Lilly

This is nuts, but I don't care.

Breaking our kiss, I pull back as much as I can, trapped between Z's hard body and his truck.

"What's wrong, all your club whores go home for the holidays?"

He smirks, but a muscle tics at the corner of his eye. Maybe I offended him?

"Jealous, sexy girl?"

I flatten my palms over his chest with the intention of pushing him away, but I get distracted by the rock-hard muscles lurking under his warm, leather jacket.

I'm not wearing gloves, so I curl my hands, trying to warm my fingers.

He leans down, soft lips brushing against my ear. Warm breath tickling against my neck. "Come on, sexy girl, invite me in."

A shiver that has nothing to do with the cold works over me. "I already did."

"Then let's go." Reaching over me, he grabs the little brown paper bag off his roof and takes my hand,

"Wait, I've got stuff in my car that I need to bring inside."

He waits while I grab my eggnog and the plate of cookies my aunt shoved into my hands before I left.

Once we're inside, I'm oddly nervous.

Z is the only guy I've ever known who makes me nervous.

After taking off our coats, I lead him into the kitchen so I can put the nog in the fridge and the cookies on the counter. Almost shyly, Z holds out the paper bag to me.

"Condoms? You know I keep plenty of those," I joke.

He doesn't laugh.

"Open it."

When I do, I almost cry, which is stupid. Inside is a canister of Godiva dark chocolate hot cocoa mix. "I can't believe you remembered this. Where did you manage to find it?"

He shrugs casually, but his smile and the crinkle at the corners of his eyes, tell me he's pleased with my reaction.

"You said it's the only kind of hot chocolate you like, and you have to have hot chocolate on Christmas Eve, it's mandatory."

"Yeah, but the Godiva store at the mall closed. Where did you even find it?"

He shakes his head. "I have my ways."

I'm not sure what to think of that. I know I'm probably reading too much into this, but the cocoa isn't easy to find, which means he went to some trouble to track down this gift. *For me.* When that's not what our relationship is about.

"Christ, Lilly, it's a beverage, not an engagement ring. Calm the fuck down."

"No, it's really sweet. Thank you."

He raises an eyebrow at me.

"You want me to make it, now?" I ask him with a laugh.

"Well, yeah. You told me it was the greatest thing ever. I gotta see if it lives up to the hype."

This is getting weird quick. Z and I fuck. We don't sit around sipping hot chocolate together.

"Okay." Rolling up my sweater sleeves, I get to work. I pull out a small saucepan, my favorite whisk, and a half-gallon of milk.

I don't bother measuring anything out. I know from memory just how much of each ingredient to use.

Z's quiet while he watches me whisk the milk and powder together over low heat. "The key is to constantly stir the milk so it doesn't burn," I tell him over my shoulder to break the silence.

"See, I would never know that. I would have jacked the fire up and set the milk to boil."

I chuckle, because I can picture him doing exactly that.

Taking down my favorite cocoa mugs, I stifle a laugh. Z's going to think I'm nuts.

At first he doesn't notice, but then he tips one mug to the side.

"Remington?"

I chuckle, a high-pitched sound that splits my ears. Why am I so *nervous* around him tonight? "They were a house-warming present from my brother. For situations just like this. You know, if I had a guy over, he'd find out quick that I've got a shotgun and a big brother."

Z throws his head back and laughs. "Yeah, I bet he's got a shovel too." He stops and looks at me a little more seriously. "He wouldn't like me at all, would he?"

"I don't know," I answer honestly. "Anyway, joke's on him. They're perfect cocoa mugs, 'cause they're so big and weighted just right. I use them all the time even though they're ugly as shit."

He chuckles as he watches me pour hot chocolate into each mug.

"No marshmallows?"

I wrinkle my nose at him. "Nope. Sorry." Stretching up on tiptoes, I snag a bottle out of the cabinet where I stash my liquor. "How about marshmallow vodka?"

His nose actually wrinkles. "Sounds a little girly."

"Suit yourself."

"Oh, all right. Hit me," he asks, holding out his mug.

After taking a sip, he glances at me. "Not bad, Lilly, you're always so clever."

I hate how much the compliment excites me. But it does. I'm used to men complimenting my looks. More specifically my boobs. But very few men ever comment on my intellect.

Z does. And it's not the first time, either. He's sincere too, which I appreciate, because it's not like he has to sweet-talk his way into my bed.

Let's face it, the man has an all-access pass.

That thick dark hair of his just begs to have my fingers run through it. His eyes are especially stunning. Mischievous midnight blue is the best way to describe them.

He smiles, softening his dangerous good looks.

"I like when you smile," I say softly.

"Oh yeah?"

"Yeah, you've got these cute little dimples." I tap his cheek to emphasis my point, and as I'm pulling away, he captures my hand.

"Cute?"

The feel of his strong hand wrapped around mine sends electrifying sensations through me. Gazing into his dark blue eyes, I'm struck by how much I really *like* Z.

"I like cute, but I also like big, dangerous, and powerful."

"Am I those things too?"

"Yes."

His eyes simmer with heat, and I use my free hand to stroke his raspy cheek. He leans in and brushes his mouth against mine. So gentle for a man who looks so demanding. Releasing my hand, he wraps his arms around my body, pulling me tight against him.

He growls when I flick my tongue against his lips and deepens our kiss. The taste of chocolate is sweet as he glides his tongue into my mouth.

ZERO

Normally I'm not into being some good girl's

bad boy experience. But despite all appearances, Lilly has never pretended to be a good girl.

Still, the fact that she finds me so dark and dangerous strokes my giant biker ego in all the right spots. Her luscious curves pressed tight against me are an extra bonus. My hands roam down to run over her perfectly round ass.

Pulling away, I take in her heavy-lidded expression. Just because I know where this night is headed, doesn't mean I don't want to enjoy the journey.

My gaze skips down to her dark green sweater. It sets off her almost-black hair and makes her green eyes appear even greener.

"You look pretty tonight."

She arches an eyebrow at me. "What?" I ask. Most girls like compliments, but you can never tell with Lilly.

"Nothing, my mother was annoyed because I didn't dress up nicer."

Stepping back, I take in her outfit more carefully. Soft, fuzzy sweater, tight enough to accent her generous curves but loose enough to still be acceptable for a night with the family. Dark jeans and low-heeled boots. Small gold earrings glitter in the kitchen light when she tosses her head back. I'm not sure what Lilly's mother expected, but *I* certainly like what the sexy girl in my arms has goin' on.

"Well, I like it," I say as my hands find their way to her cheeks, my thumbs stroking along her jaw.

"Are you planning to spend the night?" she asks.

"Are you inviting me to, or are you going to kick me out after you get yours?" I say it as a tease, but that's been the way it's gone down the last few times.

Color races up her neck into her cheeks. I had no idea Lilly was even capable of blushing.

"You can stay."

I pull her tight again and grind my hips against hers, so she knows how much I want her. "Good, 'cause I want to fuck you more than once."

"So ambitious."

CHAPTER ELEVEN

LILLY

A COUPLE KISSES from Z and I'm toast. Done.

I try sucking in a breath, but it's futile. He has me pinned against the counter. The warmth and hardness of his wonderful, muscular body sends my heart thumping wildly. His thick arms have me held captive and my panties are fucking soaked.

The heat this man stirs up inside of me is ridiculous.

And I just agreed to let him spend the night.

His face moves closer and he nuzzles my neck. His raspy cheek is rough against my skin and I love the feel. His lips brush against me, sending tingles dancing through me. Ah, God, his teeth nibbling at my ear lobe is going to be my undoing.

A soft sigh of pleasure escapes my lips and I sag against the counter for support. Too weak to even hold myself up under his sensual assault.

He chuckles against my ear. "I remember what you like, sexy girl."

Yes, he does.

His big, rough hands skim down my sides, then sneak under my sweater. "Should I undress you right here?"

He tickles my ribs but instead of laughing it makes me moan.

"Would you like me to fuck you hard and fast on your counter?"

Both hands are under my sweater but they stop just under my breasts. I make a needy pleading noise and arch my back, wanting his hands.

"Or, I could take you over to your couch. Bend you over the back and take you from behind." He punctuates the dirty image by thrusting his hips against me.

I can't take any more. I wrap my arms around his neck and tilt my head to the side, kissing him to get him to shut up. My hands stroke down his broad shoulders, over his chest, skip down over the bumps of his abs, finally landing on the impressive bulge in his jeans.

"I'll leave it up to you." I squeeze his dick just a little, so he remembers what it feels like to have my hands on him.

"I don't even know where to start, Lilly. That's how fucking nuts you make me."

It's a sweet sentiment. A little filthy too. I could get used to this sweeter side of Z. I already like his filthy side.

His lips glide over my jaw and take my mouth again. My body won't stop trembling while his hands slide down over my ass again, this time pulling me up and into him. He breaks our kiss long enough to look in my eyes. "Wrap your legs around me, girl."

"I can't."

"Yes. You. Can. Do it. I got you."

Keeping his hands under my ass he carries us into my bedroom and tosses me on my bed. It's messy and unmade, but it's not like Z has ever invited me to see his room at the clubhouse, so I really don't give a shit.

I prop myself up on my elbows to admire him. "Take your shirt off."

He grins an irresistible flash of dimples, then

slowly works his shirt off.

"Fuck," I groan.

A slower smile spreads over his face. "You like that, huh?"

Sinking my teeth into my lower lip, I can only nod. Why do I only seriously date older men again?

Money. Security. But none of that seems important as I gaze at Z's perfectly chiseled and tattooed body posing before me. Yes, he's a cocky fucker, but he's earned it. He looks damn good and I don't blame him one bit for being proud of it.

He unzips his pants and steps out of them. "Why are you still dressed?"

Kneeling up on the bed, I pull my sweater over my head and toss it at him.

"That's better. God damn your tits are perfect." He reaches to run a finger over my black, see-through bra, pausing to tease my nipples into hard points. "Fuck, that's sexy. Were you planning to get fucked tonight?" he asks with a bit of an edge to his voice.

Narrowing my eyes, I brush his hand off me. "What kind of question is that?"

He thrusts his chin at me. "The sexy underwear."

A soft chuckle escapes me. "That's all I own."

"Fuck."

"No granny panties in my drawers." I continue provoking him.

He lets out a strangled groan, while rubbing his hand over his neck and jaw. His gaze is glued to my body and a surge of feminine pride zips through me.

Hooking my thumbs under the straps of my bra, I tease them on and off my shoulders. "This is tame."

"Lilly," he warns before diving onto the mattress with me. He's all business as his hand go straight for the button on my jeans. He tugs and jerks the material down my legs, then tosses them on the floor. A conflicted look crosses his face.

"I don't know where to start first."

His sincerity makes me chuckle. "Come here and kiss me."

Very gently, he lowers himself over me. The warmth of him soaking into me. The weight of his muscular body pressing me into the mattress. One hand glides down, stroking over my panties, then pushing them aside to run his fingers over my slick folds.

One finger pushes inside and my head rolls to the side. My hips arch up, seeking more of his soft, focused, exploratory touches.

"Sexy girl's fuckin' soaked," he whispers against my ear.

I nod my head frantically. Then my whole body jerks when he scrapes his teeth over the tip of my nipple. The thin material of my bra does nothing to dull the sensation of his warm, wet mouth closing over my breast.

"Ahhh...Z."

My other breast gets the same treatment, until I'm squirming and damn close to begging for his cock.

"Z, please."

I feel, rather than see the smirk he's wearing, but he doesn't answer me, just keeps taking his sweet time licking and tasting me.

It's going to take a little more persuasion on my part, so I curl my fingers into the waistband of his boxer-briefs and tug.

"Wait," he growls.

"I can't." In this moment, I'm not ashamed at all. I'm too desperate to have his iron hard cock gliding into me to care that I'm begging.

Thankfully, he takes pity on me. Lifting his head, looking around the room as if he's as disoriented as I am, he hones in on my nightstand

and reaches to grab the condoms he knows I store in the top drawer.

There's no fumbling. Every movement is deliberate, sure and sexy as hell. He kicks out of his briefs, and hooks his arm under my knee, spreading me wide. His thumb teases against my clit, rubbing in gentle circles for a second before sliding his cock down the length of my slit. Even through the condom, I feel how hot he is. Burning up just like me. When I think I'm going to scream from frustration, he places his cock at my opening and pushes inside, so fucking slow.

The best kind of torture.

ZERO

The way Lilly stares up at me while I'm pressing inside her melting hot pussy is enough to make me lose it. But I hold on because I want this to be good for both of us. Her throaty voice in my ear is so fuckin' sexy as I pull back a bit. She's so fucking hot and wet, squeezing me so good.

I thrust in deeper and she cries out. Her sharp nails rake down my shoulders. "Harder. More. Please." Each word comes out in a sexy panting breath.

"Hang on, baby, I'm gonna give you more than you can handle."

I slide out, then thrust in harder. Over and over, jiggling her amazing tits, slamming her bed into the wall. Her nails dig in deep and I love it.

"Z, I need...I need..."

"I know. Hang on, this feels too good to stop."

But I do stop, long enough to flip us.

"Oh God, yes," her eyes practically glow in the light of the moon coming in through her bedroom window. She lowers herself onto me, so fast, she ends up gasping and raising herself right back up. I can't help chuckling.

"Easy, girl."

Lilly likes a challenge and she guides my dick into her hot pussy once more, this time easing herself down slower. Squeezing every inch of me as she takes me inside her body.

"Fuck, that's good, Lilly. Right there."

She rakes her nails down my chest and I arch up, driving my cock deeper. The primal groan she lets out makes me feel like a fucking rock star. Reaching up, I draw the straps of her bra down, freeing her perfect, round breasts, then cupping them in my hands. She throws her head back, the ends of her hair tickling against my thighs. Pinching her nipples a bit, I arch up again.

"Fuck me, girl."

She tips her head down, a lopsided smile lights up her pretty face. "Yes, sir."

Oh, fuck. "Don't start that shit." I laugh.

She lifts her body, then lowers. Rocks up and down, squeezing the fuck out of my dick. I let her have her way with me, until she's moaning with pleasure, slamming herself down and grinding her pelvis into me. "Fuuuck, that's so good, Z."

Yes it is.

I grab her hips and move her, thrusting up each time I yank her down. "Come for me, Lilly."

"I…" she never finishes. She gasps and moans. Deep, guttural moans that break apart and turn to screams. Raw, honest sounds, unlike any other woman I've ever been with.

That's it. Can't take any more. I roll her under me and pin her wrists over her head with one hand, thrusting into her hard. Her head rolls to the side, but her hips bump up to meet me thrust for thrust. Her legs tighten around my waist. Suddenly, I'm consumed with the need to have her eyes on me. I need her to see who's fucking her into oblivion.

I cup her face with one hand, turning her to me. "Look at me."

Her eyes pop open, and we stare at each other. She fights to free her hands, but I keep her pinned down. I love how she struggles beneath me and the way her eyes never leave my face. Even when she gasps again, cries out.

My cock can't take any more. I explode inside her with such force I'm surprised her head's still attached to her body. She slides into another orgasm and I keep thrusting, loving each ecstatic moan. Finally, I have to stop. I barely manage to roll over and drop the condom in the little basket by her bed.

It's Lilly who pulls me close to her body. That's new and I like it a lot. Her breath swirls across my chest. She nuzzles her cheek against me and sighs, "Merry Christmas."

CHAPTER TWELVE

LILLY

Big, warm arms hold me tight. Opening my eyes, I blink at the daylight and glance down at the heavily-tattooed arm wrapped around me.

Z.

Content, I sigh and relax against him.

"Morning," he rumbles from behind me.

Wriggling against him, I murmur my own good morning. Rough fingers trace up my arm, teasing my hair over my shoulder. His stubbly cheek rubs over my back, firm lips blaze a trail up my neck, behind my ear.

Loud thumping from the living room, startles us apart.

"The fuck?" Z snarls, reaching for his clothes and most likely a gun.

Bracing a hand on his shoulder, I listen carefully.

"Lilly!" comes the muffled shout.

Fuck!

Z scowls at me. "You expectin' someone sweetheart?"

"No."

But I should have expected this. My brother, Alex, always stops by on Christmas morning to give me a pep talk before we head to my parents'. This is the worst. He's already seen Z's truck parked in my driveway and will have a million questions for me.

Fuck.

Throwing back the covers, I scurry around the room throwing on clothes so I can go greet my brother.

ZERO

WHAT THE MOTHERFUCK?

I was about to have myself a very nice Christmas morning, sinking back inside Lilly. My cock is fuckin' throbbing at the thought. But she's racing around the room, like a nut.

'Cause there's another dude at her front door.

I don't believe this shit.

Neither of us want to be exclusive. We've had that talk. This arrangement suits me perfectly.

So why am I so fuckin' pissed right now?

At least I got here first.

Whoever's out there sounds just as pissed. Worried about my girl, I throw on my jeans and decide to put on a good show for her visitor.

I throw open her bedroom door and storm down the hallway. Bracing myself in the doorway to her living room, I feign a casual pose and assess my competition. Big, blond fucker. Well over six feet. My age, maybe older. I can handle him. Or at least get some good hits in trying.

"Lilly, darlin' I wasn't done with you yet," I slip the words out slowly, and watch the guy's face turn red with rage.

Tough shit, fucker.

Lilly gasps. "Z, dammit."

Lilly's cheeks are pink as she ducks her face into her open palms. "Fuck, fuck, fuck," she mutters over and over.

The dude's hands are fisted at his sides.

"Who is your friend, Lil?"

She finally tips her head up, glaring at the guy. "Knock it off, Alex. That's what you get for barging in without calling."

"I did call you, like a hundred times."

"Oh, shit. My cell phone's in my car."

She's hesitating. Can't blame her. As pissed as I am, I recognize this must be real fuckin' awkward for Lilly.

She glances at me again and shakes her head. "Z, this is my *brother*, Alex. Alex, this is my friend, Z."

Friend, huh. Guess it sounds better than "fuck buddy."

So this is her brother? I always pictured the dude with dark hair, like Lilly. Suddenly I'm feeling pretty fuckin' stupid standing here half-naked trying to intimidate this guy.

Her brother. Shit.

Trying to smooth over the awkward moment, I step forward and raise my hand. "Hey, Alex."

Lilly's wide, pleading eyes are clearly saying "please put some fuckin' clothes on."

Alex nods at me, but doesn't say anything.

"I, uh, I'll be right back."

CHAPTER THIRTEEN

LILLY

EVEN THOUGH I try to distract Alex by pulling him into the kitchen, his eyes bug out when Z turns around, and Alex gets a good look at the Lost Kings MC tattoo, taking up Z's entire back. While I find it incredibly sexy, Alex looks like he's going to have a stroke.

As soon as Z's out of eyesight, Alex grips my arm.

"Some motorcycle gang thug? Are you out of your fucking mind, lil' sis?"

"He's not a thug. It's a motorcycle club, *big brother*."

"Jesus fuckin' Christ. He fuckin' hurts you, I'll

kill him, and I'll have all his club brothers after me. Great."

"Knock it off. It's not like that."

I busy myself by making coffee. I'm mortified Alex caught me in this position. Not that he labors under any delusions about me, but still, this is awkward. Almost as awkward as when I found him and Sophie screwing each other after our senior prom.

"Like hell it's not. How long has this been going on? Where did you even meet someone like that?"

Now I'm pissed. He doesn't even know Z and he's judging him a little too harshly for my taste. I get the whole overprotective, big brother thing, but this is too much. Besides the awesome orgasms, Z's always been rather sweet to me. While our relationship is strictly fuck-and-go, Z never makes me feel cheap or used, something I can't say about a lot of the guys I've been with, so my brother's assumptions about Z's character based on a fucking tattoo, tick me off.

"Do you really want me to answer those questions? We hook up from time to time, does that make you happy? I met him through a friend. He's a nice guy. I like him, so stop being rude."

Alex sighs and runs his hands through his hair.

"Fine. Damn, Lilly. I just worry about you. I was worried about you last night after that shit show with Mom and Dad and Aunt Bruna's stupid mouth." He points to the box of cinnamon buns on the counter. "I brought these over to cheer you up, before we have to go back and do it all over again. I didn't expect you to have *company*."

That's our Christmas ritual—cinnamon buns and coffee before family time. Shit, if my brain wasn't in my vagina, I would have remembered.

"Sorry, he stopped by unexpectedly to bring me a present and—"

Alex quirks an eyebrow at the word present, but we're interrupted by Z returning to the room.

ZERO

Brother or not, hearing this dude hassling Lilly for being with me, makes me want to beat the shit out of him. I get it, I do. If I had a sister and found some shady dude like me in her house, I'd probably react the same way.

But she's thirty-something years old, if she wants to have a fuck buddy over, that's her business and I don't appreciate her brother trying to make her feel bad about it. Then Lilly sticks up for me.

Holy shit. I can't even say what I'm feeling hearing those fuckin' words comin' outta her mouth.

He's a nice guy. I like him—

If only she knew how *not* a nice guy I really am.

Now I'm hard as a rock, and probably shouldn't go back out there until I calm down.

When I finally make it back into the living room, I plan to head straight for the front door. "Hey, Lilly, I'm gonna—"

She glances at me with wide eyes. *Fuck.*

"Stay. Have some cinnamon buns and coffee before you go?"

My eyes skip to her brother, but he's got his back to me, busy arranging something on a plate. Probably shoving rat poison in my cinnamon bun.

"Sure, if I'm not interrupt—"

A big fuckin' smile lights up her face and I'm so done for. "You're not." She turns and bumps her brother out of the way and grabs the plate of pastries.

Setting them down on the table, she gestures for me to take a seat. It's awkward, but I snag a chair and plop myself into it, while she runs back to the kitchen. Her brother sits across from me and meets my stare head on. Brave fucker. Maybe I should ask him to prospect for us.

Inside, I'm laughing at the thought, but it must show on my face.

"Something amuse you?" Alex asks.

"Yeah, I was thinking you got big balls, throwing that attitude at a *thug* like me."

He doesn't react. Or at least he doesn't react the way I expect him to. He laughs. "I could say the same thing, you know."

"Can you guys do your whole pissing match thing some other time?" Lilly asks very sweetly as she sets out three coffee mugs and one of those insulated coffee pots on the table.

Alex pats her hand and thanks her for the coffee. At least the dude is polite to his sister.

Lilly takes her place at the head of the table and shines a beautiful smile at both of us before slipping, warm, sticky rolls on each of our plates.

"Merry Christmas, guys."

NOTES FROM AUTUMN

Anyone who knows me, knows that planning ahead of time is not a skill in my arsenal.

I'm also a master at procrastinating.

While most authors are penning their holiday stories in the middle of July, I'm pretending winter doesn't exist.

Once the snow started to fly this year, these three stories came to me. I thought about them, then set the idea aside, because I didn't have the time.

But once I mentioned the idea, people said "Yes! Do it!" and like magic, Three Kings, One Night was born.

Not quite. I labored over these three little stories, because while I have a general idea what will happen in future books, I didn't want to give anything important away. I also didn't want to write myself into a corner.

But Murphy, Wrath, and Z would not be denied.

I hope you enjoyed this little glimpse into the Lost Kings MC world.

FYI: Wrath and Trinity's full story can be found in *Tattered on my Sleeve (Lost Kings MC #4)*, *White Heat (Lost Kings MC #5)*, and *White Knuckles (Lost Kings MC #7)*. They also appear in *One Empire Night (Lost Kings MC #9.5)* and of course they are an integral part of the Lost Kings MC series overall.

Heidi and Murphy's story can be found in B*etween Embers (Lost Kings MC #5.5, More Than Miles (Lost Kings MC #6)*, and *White Lies (Lost Kings MC #15)* They are also part of *One Empire Night (Lost Kings MC #9.5)* and appear throughout the series.

Zero and Lilly's story is told in *Zero Hour (Lost Kings MC #11.5)*, *Zero Tolerance (Lost Kings MC #12)*, *Zero Regret (Lost Kings MC #13)* and *Zero Apologies (Lost Kings MC #14.)*

Thank you for reading!

Autumn

PREVIEW OF TATTERED ON MY SLEEVE

WRATH

Eight years ago...

A zap of electricity shot through me when the blonde beauty behind the bar turned her head my way. How the hell was this chick planning to keep the peace at the Blue Fox Tavern?

As long as we all behaved, the bar allowed everyone to wear their MC's colors. But it was still a biker bar. If things got out of hand, I didn't have much confidence the little cutie would be able to do much. Girl was gonna get hurt.

Once I got over the shock of seeing the new bartender, I slipped my don't-give-a-fuck face back on. My brothers, Rock and Zero, were right behind me. Brothers by *choice*. As in we belonged to the same MC. But to me, the bond we shared flowed deeper than any blood relation.

The three of us sat at the bar. The sweet, bubbly demeanor the girl approached us with was completely out of place in the seedy hangout. The way her eyes roamed over us, assessing the level of danger we posed, made me rethink my first impression.

"Hey, guys. What can I get you?"

Her gaze skipped to our cuts and zeroed in on each of our patches. She looked me over last, and holy fuck, when our eyes met, my dick perked right up. For just a second, the hard, calculating gleam in her eyes softened into something vulnerable.

The moment passed, and she swung her gaze back to Rock, whose patch read *President*.

"Scotch neat, please, sweetheart," he answered. His eyes were busy assessing her as well, but I didn't get the feeling he wanted to take her in the back room and fuck her like he did with just about every other chick he met.

As the vice president, she took Z's order next. Finally, she returned to me.

"Sergeant-at-arms, huh? The Wrecking Ball."

A slow grin spread across my face. I liked her. "I've been called worse."

"I'm sure you have. What would you like?"

I wanted *her*, spread out on the bar in front of me. "Jack Daniels, neat," I answered.

The three of us were silent while we watched her work. Slapping the drinks down with a tired smile, she glanced at the clock. She turned back to us and cocked her head, checking out our officer patches again.

"You have a shakeup in leadership? Your patches are so squeaky clean," she teased in a husky voice.

"What's your name, sweetheart?" Rock asked.

A short, excessively curvy brunette jiggled into the space behind the bar and yelped, "Trinity! I'm so sorry I'm late!"

The loud chick had herself stuffed into some sort of hot-pink tube top thing that didn't flatter her as much as she probably thought.

"It's okay, Storm," the blonde answered, even though her expression said otherwise.

Storm? Aw, fuck.

As if she heard my thought, Storm turned her big, brown, doe-eyed gaze our way and shrieked.

"Oh, Trinity! These are the guys I was telling

you about." She yanked the blonde over to us by the elbow. Her hungry gaze zeroed in on Z right away, which was unfortunate for her because he was strictly hit-it-and-quit-it.

The few times we'd met her, Rock and I had picked up a definite undercurrent of desperation with this broad. Even though we let her party at our clubhouse, we'd both been smart enough to steer clear of her bear-trap pussy.

Trinity seemed less than impressed. I wondered what sort of stories Storm had been spinning about us.

"Can I stop by after work, guys?" Storm asked.

Rock answered quick. "No. There'll be a full house tomorrow. Stop by then, hon."

Her face fell, then brightened at the invitation. I glanced down the bar at Z, who looked ready to choke our prez. I couldn't wait to give him shit later.

I finished my drink and got up to take a walk around the place. Rock's meeting was with a crew we hadn't established a lot of trust with yet. My job was to check things out before they got here. Keep the place secure. Make sure nothing happened to my president.

Back corner booth. That was where the meeting

needed to go down. As I pulled a chair over, a breathy voice behind me called out, "Hold on. I haven't cleaned that yet."

Trinity rushed over with a rag and wiped the most recent stickiness from the tabletop. I'm only human, so while she was busy cleaning, I checked out her pleasantly round ass. My fingers flexed as I imagined how perfectly her cheeks would fit my hands. For a biker chick, she was awfully conservative. I spotted what looked like two tank tops. Black on top, bright pink underneath. No thong or tramp stamp peeking out when she bent over—I think I liked that part most.

She finished and spun around. Too bad my eyes were slow to react. She definitely caught me checking out her ass. I wasn't ashamed, though, because shame's never been an emotion I wasted my time on. Besides, now my gaze was fixed on something even more exciting—her tits all pushed up and spilling out of her shirt.

It was difficult, but I looked up into her honey-colored eyes. How had I missed that color before? Or was it just the strange amber lighting we were standing under in the otherwise dark corner?

"Is Trinity a road name or your legal one?"

"Real. My mother had me during her Catholic phase."

I snorted a laugh. "How's that working out for you?"

"Well, I'm tending bar at a biker hangout, so what do you think?"

"I think things worked out well. For me, anyway."

Yeah, that one was lame. But it got a genuine smile out of her, which had been my goal.

"So, Wrecking Ball, I don't know your name."

"Wrath."

She fake-shivered and made a *brrrr* sound with her sexy-as-fuck lips. "Scary. Are you an angry fellow?"

Man, I liked this girl. She didn't say a lot, but when she spoke, she was a flirty little bitch. She clearly put up walls to keep guys like me at arm's length, and that made me want her even more.

"Not tonight. You got an ol' man?"

She scrunched up her nose. "Fuck no." Then she looked me straight in the eyes, practically daring me. "And I'm not looking for one either."

TRINITY

Wrath. His name should have been lust, because that was the deadly sin that burned through me when I looked up—way up—into his ocean-blue eyes. I should've gotten the fuck out of there. My shift was up. Storm finally had her fat, annoying ass slinging drinks. But curiosity chained me to the bar.

I should've despised bikers. I should've most definitely steered clear of this one, with his thick, muscled arms and low, sensual voice.

My normally impeccable self-preservation instinct seemed to be on the fritz.

"Well, that's good to hear. I'm not looking for an ol' lady."

"I'm not looking for a hookup either. If you don't mind, my shift is over."

Actually, I wouldn't mind a hook-up with all three of them. Maybe not the president; there was something about him that triggered a warm, brotherly memory. Which was weird because I was an only child. But the other two, yeah, I would definitely be down to—

"Trinity!" Storm yelped from behind the bar.

"Christ."

I forgot about the Wrecking Ball and stomped over to the bar.

"What?"

"I cut my hand, really bad."

As I rounded the corner, her bloody hand came into view, and I swallowed back a tidal wave of barf.

"Ew, fuck!" I whipped around and headed for the back office. "I'll go get Marky. He should probably run you to the ER."

Marky took Storm to the hospital, and I got stuck behind the bar for the rest of the night. Wrath and his friends met with an even scarier group of thugs. But they didn't cause any trouble and they ignored me, so I didn't care.

"Trinity?"

I looked up to find the president staring at me.

"Have you heard from Storm? She okay?"

I shook my head. It was unlikely I'd hear from Storm or Marky. "Nothing yet."

He nodded once and tipped his head to the side. "You hang with any local MCs?"

He was asking if I was club ass for one of his rivals. Surprisingly, I wasn't offended. "No."

"Oh, you just seemed familiar—"

"My dad was in the Silver Saints when I was a kid."

Sympathy shone in his gray eyes. Clearly, he

knew their rep. Fuck, why did I even tell him that? I usually kept that shit to myself.

"He still in?"

"He's dead."

He quirked an eyebrow at me as if he wanted me to continue, and for some strange reason, I did.

"He died in prison when I was ten."

"Club take care of you and your mother?"

A shiver of revulsion rippled over me, and I closed my eyes for a second. Yeah, they'd taken care of us all right.

"Not really."

He nodded as if he wasn't surprised.

His VP called to him. He quickly scribbled on one of the napkins. "Here's the address and number for our clubhouse. We're working on moving into a bigger place, but this is it for now. Stop by tomorrow night if you want. At the door, tell them Rock invited you."

"How many patched-in brothers you got, Rock?"

"Ten right now."

"Small."

"Yeah. Like you said—had a shakeup in leadership. Later, Trinity."

I watched him walk away. Like fuck was I going

to any club party. I didn't care how "hot" or "nice" they were—according to Storm.

I looked at the address. Right next door to a strip club. Big surprise there.

"You closing soon?" The Wrecking Ball was back.

"Yeah, thank fuck. My feet are killing me."

He threw back his head and laughed, a deep, sexy, rumbling chuckle. Curling his hands over the side of the bar, he swung his upper body over to check out my shoes. "At least you're wearing sneakers and not fuck-me pumps like Storm. Can I buy you a drink, Trinity?" he asked in a much more serious tone.

"I don't drink on the job."

He gave me a curt nod, and I took the trash into the back room. Marky could deal with it later.

WRATH

I'd waited an hour for Trinity to disappear long enough for me to hustle her straggling customers out the door. The three of us agreed we'd stay until closing since Trinity was all by herself. But the poor girl looked ready to drop, so the bar was closing early.

"Oh, did everyone leave?" Her soft voice pulled me away from my staring contest with a bottle of Jack Daniels. I pushed it away.

"Yup."

"Even your guys?"

That bugged me for some reason. I'd seen her chatting with Rock earlier. "Yeah, why?"

She shrugged as if she'd only asked to be polite and didn't really care one way or another.

"Anything else you need to do?"

"No, fuck it, I already worked way over my shift."

I chuckled at that. She punched her time card and stood there watching me.

"Do you leave by the back door or something?"

She laughed. "No, nothing but a dark, dirty, scary alleyway."

"Can I give you a lift home?"

Her gaze drifted to mine and a mischievous little gleam shone in her eyes. "Do you have your bike?"

"Of course." What a ridiculous question.

"Sure, you can give me a ride."

On the surface, her words were innocent, but she made them sound dirty. Or maybe it was my dick's wishful thinking.

My baby was parked right outside. Trinity

studied it for a minute before looking up at me. "Do you have an extra helmet?"

"Actually, I do." I liked to be prepared when picking up chicks.

I dug it out and handed it over. She fiddled with it for a minute, then strapped it on like a pro.

The night was chilly, and I wished I had something to offer that would cover her better than the skinny little straps of her tank top. "You're going to be cold. I'm sorry. I don't have a sweatshirt or something with me."

"I'll be okay."

She got on behind me like she'd done it a million times.

"Have you been on a bike before?"

A soft chuckle and her warm breath swept over the side of my neck. "Yeah, I've ridden."

I started her up, twisted the throttle a few times, and took off. After a few blocks, Trinity's hands moved from my hips to my front as she wrapped her arms around me. The distinctive movement of her hand inching toward my cock distracted me for a moment. What the hell was she up to?

When I finally stopped at a red light, I turned my head to shout, "Where are we going?"

"751 Mason Street."

Mason Street. Why did that sound familiar? "That's three doors down from the bar!"

"I know. I wanted a ride."

I shook my head and took the long way back to Mason Street. Maybe she wasn't as indifferent to my charms as she seemed.

Surprisingly, the spot I vacated was still open, so I slid in there. She handed me the helmet and ran her hands through her hair a few times. I don't think she did it on purpose, but she looked damn sexy. I still straddled my bike because she hadn't invited me in yet.

"Aren't you going to walk me home?"

Hell. Yeah.

I scanned the quiet street, searching for 751. It really was almost right next to the bar.

It was also a shithole.

"That's convenient," I said, nodding at the Blue Fox.

"Happy accident."

She had her keys in her hand, and we stood there staring at each other. She seemed to be trying to come to a decision. I'm a patient guy. I could wait.

"Do you want to come in? I can make you a biker's poison."

I tried really hard not to get all cocky about the invite. "What's that?" I asked, reaching out to tuck a few strands of wild hair behind her ear. Her eyelids fluttered at my touch. I was getting to her. The urge to do some sort of touchdown dance hit me.

"It's Jack and rum. Shake it and shoot it."

My lip curled in disgust. "Gross. Why ruin Jack like that?"

"I knew it. Knew you were a whiskey snob."

She was actually teasing me and joking around. I wanted to kiss her.

"Come on. I'll find something else for you."

If the outside of the building looked bad, inside was a fucking nightmare. This coming from a guy who hung out in a clubhouse with nine other male pigs. Rickety stairs led up to an even more questionable landing.

She opened the first door.

Inside wasn't so bad. It was tiny but clean. What little she had was organized and pretty.

"Do you want a beer?"

"Sure."

My big shit-kicking boots felt strange in her tiny little apartment. But toeing them off might give her the wrong impression. I threw myself onto her couch and sank down so fast I wondered if I'd ever get out of it.

She returned and handed me a bottle of beer.

"Thanks. I think you're done serving for the night now."

A small smile played over her lips. After a beat or two, she tucked herself onto the couch. Not really next to me, but not so far away I couldn't reach out and run my finger down her arm.

"So, Wrath, what do you do besides the sergeant-at-arms stuff?" She flicked her hand in the air like the topic bored her.

Huh. She was the first chick who hadn't wanted to sit and discuss the MC for hours on end.

"I fight."

She rolled her eyes at me. "So predictable."

"No really. Mixed martial arts style."

"Are you any good?"

"I'm undefeated."

"Doesn't the MC take a lot of time away from training?"

I considered her question carefully before answering. Yes. Actually, the last two years had been nothing but battle after battle within our club. I'd had very little time to focus on training or fighting. I hadn't needed anywhere else to redirect my rage though, either.

"Yeah, sometimes."

"So if you're undefeated, shouldn't I have heard about you?"

"MMA isn't legal in New York, so these are underground fights."

"So what else do you do?"

Fuck chicks, ride my bike, knock people out.

"Saving to get my own gym."

Suddenly, she was right next to me. Her hand brushed over my cheek.

"What do you like to do, Trinity?"

"Read."

"That's not very exciting."

"Trust me, I've had enough excitement in my life." Her voice came out more pained than teasing. There was that vulnerability I glimpsed in the bar.

I turned to face her, cupped her cheek, and ran my thumb over her soft skin. She pushed forward and tentatively pressed her lips to mine. I reached behind me to set the beer on the end table, then placed my hand on the other side of her face.

She yelped and bolted backward. "Cold hand!"

"Sorry."

Unruffled, she swooped in and kissed me again.

Her hand dropped to my lap and she gave my cock a quick squeeze. Fuck. She had me so hard I didn't think I'd be able to get out of my jeans with a hacksaw. She rubbed harder, pressing her palm into me.

"Trin—"

I slid down a little to relieve the pressure, and she took it as an invitation to work my pants open. Sliding her hands up and down my cock. Still no words from her, though. Just kept looking at me with those fuck-me eyes. Suddenly, she dropped down on her belly, stretching her legs out behind her on the couch, and closed her mouth around my cock.

I hissed out a breath. Fuck, that felt good.

She angled and arranged herself over my lap, licking, sucking, exploring. Christ, it was amazing.

"Babe, wouldn't that be easier on your knees?" I pointed to the floor.

She released my cock with a soft pop and tilted her head toward me, her lips shiny and red.

"I don't get on my knees for anyone. Ever."

Shit. Why can't I ever keep my big mouth shut?

"Okay." I reached out and stroked her hair. My cock really wanted back in her mouth.

Her hand kept lazily working up and down my

shaft. Finally, she bent over and took me in her mouth again.

Sweet motherfucking heaven. I couldn't help thrusting up, and she didn't seem to mind. She made happy little humming noises that vibrated up and down my dick.

"Trinity, honey. I'm close. Fuck, I'm gonna blow. Stop now if you don't want me shooting in your mouth, babe."

Please don't stop. Please don't stop.

She paused, and for an awful second, I thought she was going to stop. I froze, waiting, but then she took me deeper, trailing her tongue along the underside of my cock where she apparently realized I was extra sensitive.

My fist curled in her hair. I really wanted to see her fucking eyes but couldn't from this position. Then she took me all the way to the back of her throat. All thought left. White lightning gathered in my sac, streaking up until I came with painful intensity. Trinity didn't stop. She sucked and swallowed while keeping her plush lips wrapped around my cock.

"Ah, fuck! Trin. Shit."

She kept licking and kissing. Finally, she stopped and looked up with a soft smile.

I cupped my hand behind her neck and pulled her to me. "Thank you."

I tried kissing her, but she wriggled away. "Guys don't like that after doing that."

Huh?

She sat up and reached over to take a sip of my beer. Christ, my spent cock jumped when she put the bottle to her lips. She set the bottle down and crawled into my lap. With one hand at the back of her head and one above her ass, I pressed her against me and took her mouth hard. Forcing my tongue in her mouth, I explored every inch. I wasn't nearly done with this little angel. No fucking way. I slid my hands down to cup her ass. Just as I'd suspected, my palms curved perfectly around each cheek. Holding her tight, I powered off the couch. She held on and let out a little squeal.

"Bedroom?"

She giggled and jerked her head in the only possible direction the bedroom could be. Yeah, she'd sucked my brain out through my cock.

I shuffled us in there, even with my pants falling down.

The fuck?

A pink, frilly twin bed and some cheap furniture

were all she had in here. I set her down gently, and she scooted up onto the mattress.

I took a moment to zip up, but left everything else undone because I planned to fuck her very soon.

"Get those pants off, babe."

She stood and tried to push past me. I held her with one arm. Tilting her head up, I searched her face. "That wasn't enough, angel eyes."

Tattered on My Sleeve (Lost Kings MC #4) is available for purchase at all your favorite retailers. Click **here** to purchase!

THE LOST KINGS MC® WORLD

by USA Today bestselling author
Autumn Jones Lake

*This is my suggested chronological reading order
for all of the books in the Lost Kings MC World.*

1. Kickstart My Heart (Hollywood Demons #1)
2. Blow My Fuse (Hollywood Demons #2)
3. Wheels of Fire (Hollywood Demons #3)
4. Renegade Path (A Lost Kings MC World Novel)
5. Slow Burn (Lost Kings MC #1)
6. Corrupting Cinderella (Lost Kings MC #2)
7. Three Kings, One Night (Lost Kings MC #2.5)
8. Strength From Loyalty (Lost Kings MC #3)
9. Tattered on My Sleeve (Lost Kings MC #4)
10. White Heat (Lost Kings MC #5)

11. Between Embers (Lost Kings MC #5.5)

12. Bullets & Bonfires (A Lost Kings MC World Novel)

13. More Than Miles (Lost Kings MC #6)

14. Warnings & Wildfires (A Lost Kings MC World Novel)

15. White Knuckles (Lost Kings MC #7)

16. Beyond Reckless (Lost Kings MC #8)

17. Beyond Reason (Lost Kings MC #9)

18. One Empire Night (Lost Kings MC #9.5)

19. After Burn (Lost Kings MC #10)

20. After Glow (Lost Kings MC #11)

21. Zero Hour (Lost Kings MC #11.5)

22. Zero Tolerance (Lost Kings MC #12)

23. Zero Regret (Lost Kings MC #13)

24. Zero Apologies (Lost Kings MC #14)

25. Swagger and Sass (Lost Kings MC #14.5)

26. White Lies (Lost Kings MC #15)

27. Rhythm of the Road (Lost Kings MC #16)

28. Lyrics on the Wind (Lost Kings MC #17)

29. Diamond in the Dust (Lost Kings MC #18)

30. Crown of Ghosts (Lost Kings MC #19)

31. Throne of Scars (Lost Kings MC #20)

32. Reckless Truths (Lost Kings MC #21)

33. Rust or Ride (Lost Kings MC #22)

...and many more to come!

ACKNOWLEDGMENTS

There are so many people I want to thank. Everyone who has reached out to me in one way or another—bought one of my books, recommended them to a friend, posted somewhere about the Lost Kings MC, left me a review, tweeted at me—thank you. Whether it's to tell me how much you love Rock and Hope, or how much you want a *Property of Wrath* patch, I sincerely appreciate it.

My Beta Girls, I love you guys so much. I'm always hesitant to ask for help, but each time you guys respond with such enthusiasm, I'm overwhelmed with gratitude.

Amanda, Anji, Brandy, Clarisse, Elizabeth, Krystal, Shelly, Iveta, and Robin and thank you so much for jumping right in and helping me out on such short notice.

Cara Connelly, thank you for responding with "send it over" to my panic-stricken email.

ABOUT THE AUTHOR

Autumn Jones Lake is the *USA Today* and *Wall Street Journal* bestselling author of over twenty novels, including the popular Lost Kings MC series. She believes true love stories never end.

Her past lives include baking cookies, bagging groceries, selling cheap shoes, and practicing law. Playing with her imaginary friends all day is by far her favorite job yet!

Autumn lives in upstate New York with her own alpha hero.

www.autumnjoneslake.com

facebook.com/autumnjoneslake
goodreads.com/autumnjoneslake
pinterest.com/autumnjoneslake

The End